BRAVE MOTHER BEAR

GEORGE DAVID

Copyright © 2012 GEORGE DAVID

ISBN:9798838986498

TABLE OF CONTENTS

CHAPTER ONE

In a beautiful jungle far away there lived a brave mother bear who had two cute cubs, named Nala and Lala.

Nala was the female cub and Lala was the male cub. They were so adorable. Nala was on the back of her mother while Lala was standing and waving.

CHAPTER TWO

One afternoon mother bear and her two adorable cubs were playing outside and having fun.

Suddenly, they heard a loud howling.

It was the wicked Mr Wolf who comes frequently to eat cubs when he is hungry. He immediately made his way to where mother bear and her cubs were and went straight to grab Nala but mother bear tried to fight back but was over powered by Mr Wolf and he took Nala away.

WICKED MR WOLF

CHAPTER THREE

Mother bear was so sad and angry that her cub was taken away from her so she was left with just Lala. Lala was also sad that his sister Nala had been taken away. Mother bear decided to take good care of Lala before going insearch of Nala.

CHAPTER FOUR

Nala was really tired, sad, and hungry.

Mr Wolf kept her in his house which was far away from her home and was going to eat her for dinner.

While Mr Wolf was preparing to eat her, mother bear showed up and Mr Wolf was angry.

He was about to attack mother bear and immediately, mother bear began to sing a beautiful and melodious song . She sang;

"Mr Wolf... Mr Wolf

You have a beautiful smile

A beautiful heart and a kind heart

They say you are wicked but I know you are kind.

Mr Wolf... Mr wolf

You have a beautiful smile."

As soon as Mr Wolf heard the song he fell on his knees with tears in his eyes. He felt guilty and apologized for his wrong deeds.

CHAPTER FIVE

Mother bear and her cub Nala, heads home happily to meet Lala.

When they got home mother bear rushed to were she had hidden Lala and brought him out. Nala and Lala were so happy to be reunited.

From that day, Mr wolf and mother bear became super bestfriends. And they all lived happily.

MOTHER BEAR AND HER CUBS, NALA

BRAVE MOTHER BEAR

AND LALA.

BRAVE MOTHER BEAR

17

BRAVE MOTHER BEAR